Bad Day

Sue Kassirer

Illustrated by Julia Gorton

Disney PRESS

New York

At last it was spring!

The puppies all raced outdoors. They were ready to have a good time. But one of the puppies—Wizzer—seemed to be having a bad day.

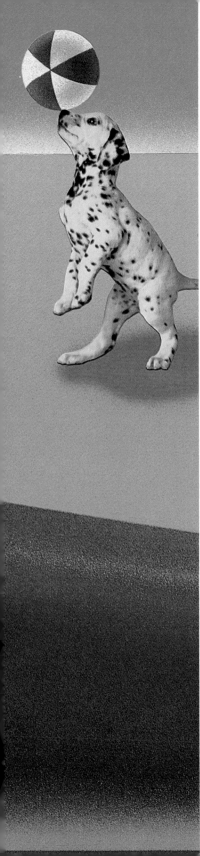

Wizzer and his brothers and sisters played in the sun on the nice soft grass. The water from the sprinkler rose high in the air and came back down with a splash—right on poor Wizzer.

"You're having a bad day," said Lucky.

"Oh, no I'm not!" said Wizzer.

As the puppies set off for a walk, each of them stepped carefully around a big muddy puddle. But Wizzer stepped right in it. SLOOP! he went, and landed flat on his back.

"You're having a bad day," said Fidget.

"Oh, no I'm not!" said Wizzer.

On the puppies strolled, down the path and past the shed. Soon Wizzer came along, knocking over a can of blue paint and covering himself from head to paw.

"You're having a bad day," said Jewel.

"Oh, no I'm not!" said Wizzer.

When the puppies arrived at the garden, they stopped to sniff the roses. But as Wizzer took in the sweet scent, a swarm of bumblebees flew out, buzzed around his head, and nearly stung him.

"You *ARE* having a bad day," said Lucky.

"Oh, no I'm not!" said Wizzer.

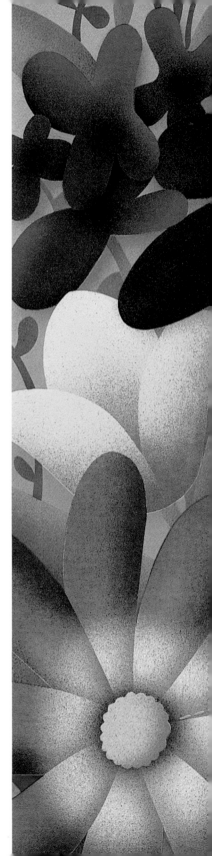

"Wizzer, why do you keep saying 'Oh, no I'm not!'?" said Fidget. "You got sprayed by the sprinkler, you slipped in a puddle, you were covered in blue paint, and a swarm of bumblebees nearly stung you. Surely that's a bad day!"

"Oh, no it's not," said Wizzer.

"First I had the most
refreshing bath.

"Then I saw an amazing cloud. It looked just like a giant dog biscuit!

"I had the time of my life decorating the path.

"And the most beautiful music
buzzed right around my head."

All of his brothers and
sisters looked at Wizzer with
big wide eyes. They had never
known that a bad day could be
so much fun.

"Wizzer," said Jewel, "it
looks as if your bad day has
been the best day of all!"

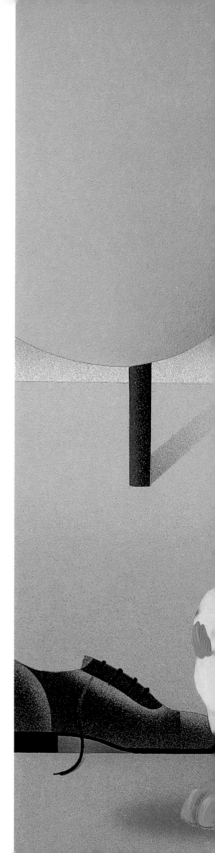

"Oh, yes
it has!"
said Wizzer.

For Bunny and Pooch
—S. K.

To my sister Mary and my brother John,
with whom I spent many spring days exploring our
seemingly endless backyard
—J. G.

Printed in the United States of America.

First Edition
1 3 5 7 9 10 8 6 4 2

Library of Congress Card Number: 96–86096
ISBN: 0–7868–3127–8

The artwork for each picture is prepared using photographs and airbrushed acrylic on paper.

This book is set in 32–point Smile.

Designed by Julia Gorton.

Based on characters from the book, *101 Dalmatians*, by Dodie Smith, published by Viking Press.